WRITTEN BY
MICHAEL DAHL

ILLUSTRATED BY
LEO AQUINO

GOODNIGHT SKATEBOARD

CAPSTONE EDITIONS
a capstone imprint

The sun is rolling across the sky.

The wind blows fast.

The clouds race by.

We bike to the park on this bright afternoon.

The skateboard contest will start very soon!

Big Brother signs up
with the neighborhood crew.

We wish him good luck,
then find seats with a view.

The skaters line up.

Brother zooms
down the stairs.

Then he crouches . . . he leaps!

Wow! He catches some air.

Skaters swerve on the ramps.

They grind on the rails.

They fly up the bowls
and grab onto their tails!

We hear the wheels sing
as Brother and friends
race the obstacle course
through its boxes and bends.

Brother scores on the half-pipe.

His wheels stay on track.

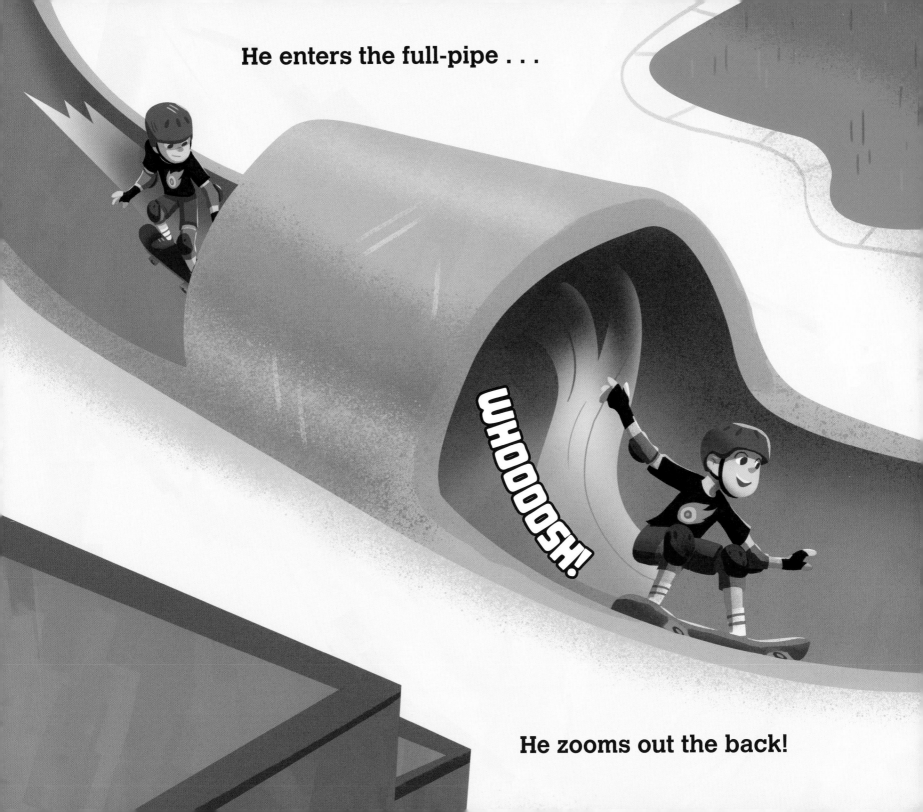

The crowd jumps and shouts.

Brother holds up his deck.

A blue and gold ribbon is placed round his neck!

Then the park lights snap on.

The music dies down.

Now it's time for goodbye,
time to bike back through town.

Goodnight to the kids and the moms and the dads.

Goodnight to the helmets, the gloves, and the pads.

Goodnight to the skaters
who flipped and who flew.

Goodnight to the half-pipes and bowls they zoomed through.

Goodnight to the streets
and the alleys we pass.

Goodnight to our neighbors.
We reach home at last.

Brother hands me his medal.

"Just practice and wait.
It's good luck," he explains,
"when it's *your* turn to skate."

In your dreams ride a ramp,
then soar out of sight.

Fly high, skateboard . . .

Sleep well and goodnight.

Published by Capstone Editions, an imprint of Capstone
1710 Roe Crest Drive, North Mankato, Minnesota 56003
capstonepub.com

Library of Congress Cataloging-in-Publication Data
Names: Dahl, Michael, author. | Aquino, Leo, illustrator.
Title: Goodnight skateboard / by Michael Dahl; illustrated by Leo Aquino.
Description: North Mankato : Capstone Editions, 2022. |
Series: Sports illustrated kids bedtime books | Audience: Ages 4–7. |
Audience: Grades K–1. | Summary: Told in rhyming text, a young
girl cheers her brother on at a skateboarding competition and returns
home with her family to dream of her favorite extreme sport.
Identifiers: LCCN 2021056982 (print) | LCCN 2021056983 (ebook) |
ISBN 9781684465231 (hardcover) | ISBN 9781684465286 (pdf) | ISBN
9781684465255 (kindle edition)
Subjects: LCSH: Skateboarding—Juvenile fiction. | Skateboarding—
Competitions—Juvenile fiction. | Brothers and sisters—Juvenile fiction. |
Stories in rhyme. | CYAC: Skateboarding—Fiction. | Contests—Fiction. |
Brothers and sisters—Fiction. | Stories in rhyme. | LCGFT: Stories in rhyme.
Classification: LCC PZ8.3.D136 Gr 2022 (print) | LCC PZ8.3.D136 (ebook) |
DDC [E]—dc23
LC record available at https://lccn.loc.gov/2021056982
LC ebook record available at https://lccn.loc.gov/2021056983

Designer: Hilary Wacholz

Printed and bound in the USA. PO4882